CW00551458

NEW GIRL

Copyright © 2015 by Carina Sanfey

All rights reserved.

First published in 2015 by Indigo
Lagoon Publications Limited, London.

No part of this publication may be
reproduced in whole or in part by any
means, including electronic, mechanical,
photocopying, recording or otherwise,
or stored in information storage and
retrieval systems, without prior written
permission from the publisher.

NEW GIRL

Sarah Reilly, Zombie Killer

Book 1

Carina Sanfey

Indigo Lagoon Publications

Prologue

Since the dawn of the human race, people have lived and people have died. Some have lived long, some less, but most, once dead, remained in the ground; that is, those untouched by the Sleeper.

The original Sleeper is said to have been an Abyssinian woman who died in a fire some five thousand years ago; the blaze was tinged with magic, and thus she awoke once buried and began to wage her war on the living. Once a dead person becomes one of the undead, their essence is gone and they become a beast, a demon; while they physically resemble they whose body they have taken (although they have far more brute strength) and they share their memories, they are not the same person.

New Girl

The Sleeper, through incantations, may resurrect the dead, and these dead become the Awakened, soulless beings hell-bent on the destruction of the living. The only way the Awakened can be killed (and this includes the Sleeper) is by beheading. Once the Sleeper has been killed, the last person she or he resurrected becomes the new Sleeper and gains the power to raise the dead; thus, the cycle continues indefinitely. If the slain Sleeper has not yet awakened anyone, the previous Sleeper's penultimate victim has the dubious honour of being the new Sleeper, and so on and so forth.

For over four hundred years, the original Sleeper and her successors, whose sole visible feature separating them from ordinary people is the blue glow that emanates from them by daylight, waged unabated war on the living with their army of dead, until an Egyptian sorcerer

known only as 'Nam' created an
incantation to give to ordinary people
power that would help them succeed
against the Awakened. He enchanted
one hundred and twelve weapons,
pairing each with a set of incantations,
and these incantations were used to give
one hundred and twelve young women
the ability to harness the power of the
sword. When each one died, their sword
was retaken by Nam and paired with
another young woman. Nam's
incantations and responsibility for these
people and their weapons were passed
down through his descendants, his
successor each time becoming the new
Nam.

The Awakened will never be stopped,
but these women, the Killers of the
Undead, are the only ones who can slow
their relentless onslaught against the
living. Without them, the world is
doomed.

Chapter 1

It was a small graveyard, one which had been out of use for close to a century, though the Sleeper could tell that there were many hundreds of bodies here. Crumbling tombstones dotted the overgrown field, some sunken and half-buried in the ground, but she sensed that most of the bodies lay beneath the unmarked stones and makeshift crosses. Her journey to these shores had been long and arduous, but at last she had reached that famed island, that place no Sleeper had ever penetrated, that land that had never known the wrath of the Awakened. Now was her chance to wreak a whole new level of destruction, to go down in history as one of the greatest Sleepers ever to raise the dead. She had been in this role for three years and in that time had awakened more than five thousand of those who had gone before, but this project was her biggest task yet. Taking the ferry from the continent to this island unnoticed had been no mean feat for one who glowed blue by daylight.

New Girl

She started the process at the southeasternmost corner of the graveyard and spiralled in towards the centre with the intention of awakening all who lay there, save those who had been too young at their time of death to be of any use to her. It would take them several hours to awaken and claw their way out of their graves, which was why she had started her task at the earliest possible hour and why she had chosen such a totally abandoned graveyard. There were other graveyards in this parish, but they were all still in use, still frequented by the locals. Anyone buried here was long since forgotten.

As always, she didn't know what sort of state her new army would be in when they arose, and it was safe to assume that around thirty to fifty percent would be unusable due to either highly visible mortal wounds or marks of pestilence. She would do away with those straight away and put their skeletons back in the ground; she needed servants who could blend in with the living, at least after dark.

New Girl

The process of resurrecting the dead was tiring, but she was experienced at it by now. She worked through the pain, through the exhaustion, until eventually she had been around the entire graveyard. She was just starting to hear stirring from the first graves she had done, and she stood and waited patiently for her followers to rise.

The first grave was a much-used family plot with nineteen inhabitants, but unfortunately thirteen had died of a highly visible pox and were thus of no use to her; she swiftly beheaded them and examined the remaining six; four men and two women, aged, perhaps, between twenty and forty at the time of their death.

"Who do you serve?" she asked calmly.

"We serve you," the six intoned.

"Excellent," she said, "Now, stay put. I have work to do; I need to raise our army."

None of the six said anything further; freshly-raised Awakened were always somewhat dazed for the first couple of days. Their personalities and thoughts would begin to emerge then, and she could assess their strengths and weaknesses before appointing a leader to this particular group and moving on. She planned to wreak havoc all over this island, and she wanted to get her business here wrapped up within the month. She intended to lie low for the winter somewhere in the Iberian peninsula, and she would have to leave plenty of time for her return journey.

She continued on through the graveyard, visually assessing everyone she had awakened and culling those whom she could not use. It appeared this parish had been struck by many disfiguring pestilences over the centuries, not to mention a few extremely gory fights, and she was left with a paltry 197 out of the 421 she had raised.

"Come with me," she called, "It's time to go to your new home."

She had already picked out a place, and it was close by enough that they didn't even need to venture onto any of the roads. It was a relatively large disused, abandoned farmhouse, and as far as she could tell nobody had any stake in it; the half-hinged front door had been so thick with cobwebs that she surmised it hadn't been entered in decades, possibly even close to a century. She led her new followers over fences and through fields until they arrived at the house, and she gently pushed open the slightly-broken door, remaining by the entrance, counting all of the Awakened to ensure they were all still with her. It wouldn't do to lose any of them at this early stage; she wanted them all to fully awaken in her presence, thus giving her the best chance of having their complete trust. There were still plenty of things that could go wrong, of course, but she had been in this business long enough to accept that raising an army of undead was not without its risks. Overall, the benefits generally outweighed the pitfalls, although there had been one former follower of hers who had caused several months of trouble for her in Novosibirsk two years previously. Since then, she had been more careful to keep track of her new recruits for at least the first month. That nasty business could have been prevented had she been more vigilant from the outset.

New Girl

Once they were all inside, she went in and closed the door behind her. Her new followers were milling around in the large, old-style kitchen they had entered, still dazed and confused, interacting neither with her nor with each other.

"Lie down," she called out, "Get some sleep."

Stiffly and awkwardly, they began to lie down on the hard stone floor, some spilling into the next room, and she watched for hours as they began to gradually relax, to seem less stiff, more human, more natural.

She smiled to herself. It had begun.

Chapter 2

The tall, blonde sixteen-year-old girl standing outside the gates of Ballynavolan Community School in County Meath didn't blend in with any of the other teenagers going into the grounds; for one thing, she was wearing considerably less clothing than any of them. Sarah Reilly had been defiantly opposed to the idea of moving to a new home and a new school, and she had defied her parents that morning by wearing the outfit she thought would irk them the most; a super-short red plaid skirt and a white belly top, topped off with perilously high black stilettos. Now that she stood alone outside her new school, though, that didn't seem like such a wise choice. The other girls mostly wore jeans and t-shirts, and those wearing skirts or dresses wore considerably longer ones. Sarah was certainly the only one with her belly showing. As for the boys, they mostly looked as though they had just stumbled out of bed and grabbed the first un-ironed thing they could find. Suddenly, Sarah found herself longing for the disgustingly green uniform of her old school. At least she had blended in there.

There was nothing she could do now; she would have to go in and face the horrors of being not only the new girl, but the inappropriately-dressed new girl. She took her sweatshirt out of her schoolbag and tied it around her waist. It almost covered the bare skin, but not quite.

Hyper-aware of her poor choice of shoes, Sarah walked awkwardly through the open iron-wrought gates and looked around. The school consisted of four separate two-storey stone buildings, two on her left and two on her right, and there was a large green area, complete with two gigantic oak trees and several picnic benches, in the middle of the campus where some students were milling about. She looked around, lost. There was nothing to indicate where she should go. She stopped dead and was immediately pushed forward; she turned around to see that she'd been caught up in a group of older boys.

"Check out the new girl!" hollered one of them mockingly, "Did you forget your clothes?"

Sarah turned beetroot-red and said nothing. The group of boys passed, still laughing and jeering at her. Looking around, it seemed as though everyone was staring at her, and she wanted nothing more than to drop into a hole in the ground.

The 200-pupil school was much smaller than her school in Dublin had been, but it seemed like more of a jungle, more of a minefield. She didn't know anyone, and

New Girl

she was a total outsider, her accent marking her as different. She hadn't had to speak yet, but she dreaded the moment when she would.

"Are you Sarah Reilly?"

She spun around to see a tall, pencil-thin, middle-aged balding man wearing a navy suit and glasses that seemed to teeter at the end of his long nose.

"Yeah, that's me," she said.

"I'm Mr Keegan, the principal," said the man, looking her up and down, "I see you didn't bother to read the dress code."

Sarah blushed and said nothing.

"Just because we don't have a uniform it doesn't mean you can wear what you like, young lady. Anyway, come with me, I need to have a chat with you before you get started."

New Girl

Wordlessly, Sarah followed Mr Keegan, whom she had already decided she intently disliked. The tall man led her into the first building on the left and then into a stairwell on the right; once at the top of the stairs, Sarah found herself on a long corridor.

"My office is here on the left," said Mr Keegan, opening a door, "Please, step in."

Sarah's first impression of Mr Keegan's office was that it matched his dull personality very well indeed. There were no pictures, no photographs, nothing on the wall other than degree certificates and a blank year planner. The man's desk held only a computer, a pad of paper and a sparsely-furnished pencil-holder, and there was one chair behind the desk and two in front. Other than the desk and chairs, the only furnishings were a bookcase filled with old yearbooks and a file cabinet.

New Girl

"Do you like living here so far?" asked Mr Keegan in what was clearly a terrible attempt at seeming friendly.

"Yeah, yeah, it's great," lied Sarah, who so far detested rural life.

"Your old school sent over your results and your report cards," continued Mr Keegan, ignoring Sarah's words, "It seems you're a bright student who is averse to doing any work, is that correct?"

Sarah blushed again.

"I suppose," she said cautiously, hoping it wasn't a leading question.

"Well, that won't do here," said Mr Keegan, "Here, we expect every student to reach and exceed their full potential." Sarah had a feeling that this was the speech given to every student on their first day; she wondered just how she was supposed to exceed her full potential if it was, indeed, her full potential.

New Girl

"I'll be expecting better from you, Sarah," continued Keegan, "And don't forget, fifth year is just as important as sixth year, if not more. It's where the foundation is laid, and a poorly-laid foundation makes for an unstable building!"

Sarah couldn't think of anything to say that was vaguely appropriate, so she said nothing. As a rule, she wasn't fond of metaphors, and she felt Mr Keegan had definitely taken this one a little too far.

"Here's a copy of the school rules for your perusal," said Mr Keegan, producing a sheet out of nowhere, "Please pay close attention to section five, that's where the dress code is detailed. Do you have all your books?"

Sarah nodded.

"Excellent. Your first class will be in your form room with your year head, go back down the stairs and into the first classroom on the right, marked room G48."

With that, Mr Keegan stood up and marched to the door, holding it open expectantly. Sarah exited, suddenly conscious again of what she was wearing, and made her way back down the stairs.

She checked her watch; it was 08:40; five minutes until class started. She located the correct classroom, opened the door and walked in.

It seemed as though all eyes were on her as she walked to the one free seat, which was, naturally, front and centre. The teacher hadn't arrived yet, and the chatter and raucous laughter of Sarah's thirty-two fellow fifth-year students was almost unbearably loud. She kept her eyes down as she took her seat and placed her schoolbag on the floor, still

New Girl

tightly clutching the rule sheet Mr Keegan had given her.

The door opened again only seconds after Sarah had sat down, and the hubbub settled to a quiet whisper as a short, rotund, elderly woman walked in.

"Good morning, boys and girls!" she said over-enthusiastically. There was no reply.

"I'm your year head this year, of course," she continued, "and you'll still have me for English."

Sarah thought she heard the sound of several faint groans coming from around the classroom, but the jolly teacher appeared to be oblivious to these reactions.

"And, of course, we have a new student with us today!" she continued, staring right at Sarah with an enormous and terrifying smile on her face, "Sarah,

New Girl

would you like to stand up and tell us a bit about yourself please?"

That was, of course, the last thing Sarah wanted to do, but she didn't appear to have any choice in the matter, so she awkwardly stood up and turned around to face her peers, not daring to look any of them in the eye but instead fixing her gaze on a spot of dirt on the back wall.

"I'm Sarah," she mumbled, "and I'm from Dublin and I'm sixteen and I've just moved here."

She hurriedly sat back down, and the room was filled with an awkward silence.

"Great!" said the teacher, whose name Sarah still did not know.

Sarah didn't manage to keep listening to the teacher for long; her voice was constantly enthusiastic to the point of extreme boredom on the part of the

New Girl

listener, and she placed what Sarah thought was far too much emphasis on 'school spirit'. Sarah soon found herself struggling to keep her eyes open, and she began to blink furiously in an effort to keep herself awake. She took in very little of what the round little woman said, and noticed at some point that timetables and journals had appeared on all their desks. When the bell rang some forty minutes later, she wasn't entirely sure what she was supposed to be doing. Everyone else seemed to be getting ready to leave, so she stood up and picked up her bag, turning around and promptly bumping into a tall brunette wearing a knee-length blue dress that emphasised both her large breasts and small waist.

"Watch where you're going," said the girl, giving Sarah a dirty look and pushing past her. She was immediately followed by a red-haired boy, who gave Sarah the same sort of denigrating look as his friend had. Sarah couldn't help but feel as though she had just made two enemies without saying a word.

The last of the students were now trickling out of the room, and Sarah hurriedly followed them, not having any idea whether or not they were all supposed to be going the same way. The corridor was filled with students of all ages, and she kept a close eye on the green schoolbag of one of the boys she knew to have exited the same classroom as her, following him back outdoors and across the grounds to one of the buildings on the opposite side.

It was only when she saw him slip around a corner and take out a cigarette and a lighter that she realised he definitely wasn't going to class.

Cursing her inattentiveness, Sarah turned around; the outside area was now almost deserted, and she had absolutely no clue where she was supposed to be going.

New Girl

She looked at the timetable in her hand; she was supposed to be in maths, in room L6, but that meant nothing to her. She didn't even know in which of the four buildings she was meant to be.

"Sarah Reilly?"

The male voice came from behind her; she was going to get in trouble with Mr Keegan. She turned around slowly, wincing, but it wasn't Keegan; it was another man, shorter, rounder, older, more dishevelled and with an old-fashioned grey beard and handlebar moustache.

"Yeah," said Sarah, "Sorry, I got lost... are you a teacher?"

"No," said the man, some kind of foreign accent apparent in his voice, "I'm here to tell you of your destiny."

Sarah blinked.

New Girl

"What?" she asked, assuming she had misheard.

"You've been called," continued the man in a calm and placid tone that really didn't match his words. He took a large bottle of something clear and sparkling out of his pocket and unstoppered it.

"Called... where? What?" asked Sarah, becoming more and more confused and starting to think it might be prudent to run away.

The man threw the contents of the bottle over Sarah, soaking her thoroughly, all the while intoning foreign and strange words. Sarah was stuck to the spot with shock and fear for a minute or so, and then she ran.

Chapter 3

Sarah didn't look back as she ran, and she fervently hoped the strange man wasn't following her. She ducked in a side door to one of the school buildings and didn't stop running through the empty corridors until she had found a bathroom.

She locked herself inside a cubicle and stood with her back to the door, trying to catch her breath. She had no idea what had just happened. Who had that man been, and what had he done to her? She was soaked in that stuff. It smelled like incense or something, only stronger, and it made her feel quite nauseous.

Once she had composed herself somewhat, she exited the cubicle and went to assess the damage in the mirror. She looked as though she'd been splashed by a passing car, but the smell

New Girl

was the main problem. Hurriedly, she put her schoolbag down on the floor and pulled off her top, rinsing it under the hot tap in the sink before wringing it out and sticking it under the hand-dryer.

She almost jumped out of her skin when she heard the creak of the door opening, and she hurriedly tried to put her still-damp top back on, but she wasn't quick enough. The girl in the blue dress from earlier had walked in, and she was followed by the red-haired boy.

The girl raised her eyebrows at the sight of Sarah half-naked, and the boy started to snort with laughter.

"Get out of here!" squeaked Sarah at the boy, "This is the girls' bathroom!"

"You weren't wearing enough clothes to start with, love," said the girl as she made her way over to one of the sinks, taking a tube of deep red lipstick out of her pocket, "What are you doing skipping your first ever class here, anyway?"

"I got lost," admitted Sarah, "and then some madman outside poured water all over me."

"A madman? Cool. What'd he look like?"

"Old. He had a beard."

"Weird. You're Sarah, right?"

"Yeah."

"I'm Liz, and this here is Dónal. Don't worry about him, he practically lives in the girls' bathroom. You should probably put your top back on, though, in case he gets too excited. Sorry about earlier, by the way. I didn't mean to snap at you."

"That's okay," said Sarah, starting to feel slightly relieved. She wasn't sure whether or not she liked Liz, but it seemed as though she could be a potential friend, and that was something she very much needed right now.

"Dónal," said Liz, "Go into a cubicle for a minute while I get Sarah cleaned up."

Dónal did as he was told, Sarah pulled off her skirt and the two girls set about rinsing her clothes and drying them using the hand-dryer; five minutes later, Sarah was vaguely respectable again.

"Come on," said Liz as Dónal exited the cubicle, "We'll take you back to class. We have Mr Moran for maths, he's cool, he won't mind that you got lost."

Sarah followed her two new friends out of the bathroom and down the corridor, turning a corner at the end and going into a classroom filled with raucous laughter.

"Found the new girl!" called Liz loudly, and the class tittered. The relaxed-looking young man teaching the class grinned.

"Welcome," he said to Sarah, "You can only use that 'lost new girl' excuse for another week or so, make the most of it."

Sarah grinned as she sat down in the one free seat, which was directly behind the double desk Liz and Dónal were sharing and beside an orange-faced girl with peroxide-blonde hair who seemed to be paying attention to nothing but her own meticulously-pruned fingernails.

"Page seven," said Mr Moran, looking pointedly at the three latecomers, "Solve the first ten problems, please."

New Girl

Sarah took out her maths book and a copybook and began to work through the problems; maths was very much her strong suit, and she was finished within minutes. Looking around, she was somewhat smugly pleased to see that everyone else was still either scribbling furiously or massaging their foreheads while wearing looks of total confusion. She sat back in her chair and stared at Mr Moran, who was sitting down and engrossed in something on his desk.

Mr Moran was perhaps in his early thirties, and he wore a plain white shirt and navy trousers paired with an elephant-patterned tie which seemed very much out of place in a school setting. He had a full head of short black hair and faint stubble around his mouth, and his eyes were a piercing blue.

Sarah was suddenly startled as Mr Moran looked up and caught her staring at him.

New Girl

"Finished, Sarah?" he asked. She nodded, and he stood up and walked down towards her desk.

"Very good," he said after a moment's perusal, "All correct. You can go onto the next set."

Liz turned around and mouthed "clever-clogs" at Sarah as Mr Moran went back up to the top of the room, and Sarah blushed.

The rest of the period passed without incident, and Sarah was pleased to discover that their homework was what she had just been doing. She left feeling considerably more confident than she had all day, and she sidled in alongside Liz.

"Where's B07?" she asked her new friend.

New Girl

"This building, basement," said Liz, "What have you got?"

"French."

"Then, my dear, I shall see you at lunchtime," said Liz, "Dónal and I do German. Have fun, I hear Ms Bell's a hoot and a half."

Sarah wasn't entirely sure whether or not this was sarcasm, so she resolved to keep an open mind about Ms Bell as she made her way down to the low-ceilinged basement and located B07.

She was only the third person to arrive, and the teacher, a tall and slender young woman, looked up when she walked in.

"Sarah, right?" she asked. Sarah nodded.

"I'm Ms Bell," she said, "Have a seat wherever you like."

New Girl

Relieved to at last have a choice, Sarah took a seat right at the back and watched as more students filed in. She was surprised to see that they were a class of only thirteen. Life was very different in the countryside.

Sarah was quick to realise that her French was not quite up to the same standard as the rest of the students in her class, and she furiously made notes and avoided answering questions in order not to make a fool of herself. Unfortunately, she was eventually singled out.

"Sarah," said Ms Bell, "As-tu des frères ou des soeurs?"

Sarah knew this one; brothers and sisters.

"Non," she answered, relieved to be an only child.

"Ah, tu es enfant unique?"

New Girl

Had she been a unique baby? That seemed like a strange question.

"Non," she answered again, this time with a little less confidence. There were a few chuckles from the class.

"You don't have brothers and sisters, but you're not an only child?" asked Ms Bell, "Which is it?"

"Oops," said Sarah, "Sorry. Yeah, I am an only child."

"Tu es-?"

"Je suis, uh, enfant unique."

"Bon."

Sarah looked down at her copybook and fervently hoped she wouldn't be questioned again today. She definitely had some catching up to do.

She managed to get through the rest of the class without incident, and when the

New Girl

bell rang for lunch she gathered her things and stood up, setting off in the hope of finding Liz and Dónal. She didn't know where they might be, but she assumed all of the students gathered outdoors.

Once in the quadrangle, she looked around and eventually spotted Liz's blue dress; she was seated atop a picnic table, and Dónal was lounging on the bench beside it. They were alone, and Sarah hoped she wouldn't be intruding. She walked nervously over, hoping she would be welcomed.

"Sarah!" yelled Liz, spotting her as she drew closer, and Sarah smiled, relieved. She sat down opposite Dónal.

"How was French?" asked Dónal.

"Horrible," said Sarah, "German?"

"Yeah, that was pretty horrible too. Right, come on, new girl. Tell us about yourself."

New Girl

"What do you want to know?"

"Everything. Where are you living?"

"Druminnert," said Sarah, "We've only been there three days."

"Ooh, that big house that was for sale? Nice. Brothers and sisters?"

"Nope. Just me and my parents."

"Must be a change from Dublin," said Liz idly.

Sarah said nothing. She had never imagined it would be quite this different.

"So what do you do for fun around here?" she asked at length.

"There's a pub in town, McKenna's, that lets teenagers in," said Sarah, "They don't serve us drink or anything, but they let us hang out there. That's kind of it, really."

"So where do you two live?"

New Girl

"Next door to each other," said Dónal, "In Drumoolly, it's about a ten-minute walk from your house, you can walk most of the way home with us."

"Cool," said Sarah, digging into her hastily-put-together sandwich.

"Here, let's see your timetable," said Liz. Sarah handed it to her.

"Eww," said Liz, "Chemistry?"

"Hey, me too!" said Dónal.

"Losers," muttered Liz.

"And physics," continued Liz, "and art. Wow, you really are a glutton for punishment."

"What do you do?" asked Sarah.

"Easy stuff," said Liz, "Geography, biology and ag science."

New Girl

"Ag science?"

"Agricultural science," explained Liz, "Piss-easy subject. You just have to answer questions about sheep and stuff. You should've done it."

"I like my subjects," said Sarah defensively.

Liz laughed.

"I like not having to do any work," she said, "So, have you got our year group figured out yet?"

"Not even close," said Sarah, "Talk me through it."

"Well," started Dónal, clearly in his element, "There are the dumb blondes; that's Lorna, who you were sitting beside in maths, and her two cohorts, Michelle and Sinéad. They're the most irritating girls you'll ever meet, and they're pretty

New Girl

much in love with themselves. Then there are their worshippers, which is pretty much all the guys except me and Kevin. Kevin's that nerdy guy with the Harry Potter glasses who picks his nose. Then there's Fiona and Caitríona, the weirdo twins who don't talk to anyone but each other, and Marie, Deirdre and the two Ruths - they're all right, they mostly keep to themselves - and then us. And that's it."

"Wow," said Sarah, "There were a hundred and sixty in my year at my old school. I didn't even know all their names."

"Welcome to Boredomville," said Liz wryly, "You'll soon know everyone and his dog around here. Come down to McKenna's tonight, we'll be there from about seven o'clock. We'll show you around, point out everyone you need to know."

New Girl

"Sounds good," said Sarah, feeling pleased to have been invited out on her very first day.

Sarah became vaguely aware of someone shouting over the din of student chatter, and she turned around to see Mr Keegan some distance away. She could see his lips moving, but she was too far away to hear his words.

"What's going on?" she asked, nudging Liz.

"Dunno," said Liz, standing up as Mr Keegan moved through the crowds and towards them.

"All students in the assembly hall at once!" he called, "Come on, hurry up!"

"Is this normal?" Sarah asked, turning to Dónal who shook his head in reply.

New Girl

As Sarah followed Liz and Dónal and the rest of the crowd towards the building where she had started her school day, she couldn't help but feel a peculiar sense of foreboding, as though there was some connection between this and the man who had soaked her, as though the reason they were being assembled had something vaguely to do with her. She couldn't explain why she felt like this, and she knew it was irrational, but she was also absolutely certain that she was right.

Chapter 4

There were no seats in the large, dusty assembly hall, and the students sat in small groups on the floor, chattering excitedly, wondering what the occasion was. Several staff members were lined up at the top of the hall, and it was clear from their grim expressions that this was not a time for celebration; rather, something terrible seemed to have happened.

At last, Mr Keegan took his place at a hastily-erected microphone, and the noise in the hall gradually ceased. Sarah noticed two gardaí standing by the closed entrance to the hall and another one by the fire escape. This was serious.

"I apologise for the disruption to your school day, students," began Mr Keegan,

New Girl

"but two bodies have been found on campus, and the gardaí need you all to stay in here while they begin their investigation, which is, I'm sad to say, without a doubt a murder investigation. The bodies haven't been formally identified yet, but," he looked around at his fellow staff members, who all wore deeply worried expressions, "they are people who are known to all of us; Patrick and Theresa Joyce."

Gasps flew around the room, and Sarah appeared to be the only one who didn't understand the significance of the names.

"Who are they?" she whispered frantically to Liz, who had tears starting to form in her eyes.

"They run - ran - the supermarket in the village," she said, her voice heavy with shock, "They were lovely people, everyone liked them."

New Girl

Sarah somehow felt as though she were intruding on the collective grief as she watched her fellow students mourn their loss; she wasn't quite sure how she was supposed to act. She hadn't known these people, so it wouldn't be appropriate to share in the others' grief, but she still felt a sense of numb shock at the brutality, the suddenness of it all. Unbidden, the image of the man who had soaked her came to her; had he had something to do with this? Had he been the murderer? So many strange things had happened so far on her first day at this new school. Rural life certainly wasn't half as boring as she had expected it to be. She wondered should she tell someone about the man, but she realised she didn't know what she would say. There was nothing to connect him to the murder other than some strange kind of intuition on Sarah's part, and that hardly constituted grounds for an investigation.

New Girl

The next two hours passed slowly, with groups of students talking in hushed tones, teachers going back and forth to the gardaí at the doors and exchanging whispered words, and Sarah herself sitting awkwardly in the midst of all this grief and worry. At last, Mr Keegan announced that they could go home, and they filed out of the hall one by one, each having to give their name and address to the garda on the door as they went.

Sarah was glad of the company as she began to walk home; even though neither Liz nor Dónal said much, at least they were there, and three felt a lot safer than one when there was a murderer about. Sarah's new home was about a forty minute walk from the school, and she would have company for the first three quarters of it, which made her feel quite a bit better about the whole situation.

New Girl

"I wonder when the funeral will be," mused Liz.

"Did they have children?"

"Yeah," said Liz, "Three, they're all in primary school. The youngest is only six."

A lump formed in Sarah's throat, and she said nothing. Whatever about the grief at the secondary school that day, the scene at the nearby primary school must have been horrific. She wondered how someone goes about telling a small child their parents have been killed. She wanted to ask if there were other relatives who would take care of the children, but it was clear that neither Dónal nor Liz wanted to talk, so she kept quiet.

At last, they arrived at Drumoolly, and the three said their subdued goodbyes as Liz and Dónal started down the laneways to their respective farmhouses. Sarah continued to walk, her head down and her mind lost in deep, dark thoughts.

"I tried to warn you."

She looked up, startled, and saw the man who had soaked her. She jumped back instinctively.

"What do you want from me?" she asked.

"You have a destiny," he said calmly.

"Did you kill those people?" she asked, anxiety growing in her voice.

"What?" he asked incredulously, "No, no. You've got it all wrong. The Awakened killed them."

"The… who?"

New Girl

"Zombies, as your generation tend to call them."

It was becoming clear that this man's grip on reality was tenuous at best, and Sarah looked around for an escape route.

"Sarah," the man said gently, "I'm here to help you. You're the only one who can stop them. You need to find the swords; your power is in the swords."

"You're nuts," she said, "Now get the hell out of my way."

He shook his head slowly.

"I tried to warn you," he said, walking past Sarah and continuing on down the road. Sarah stood affixed to the spot for a few moments, and then continued on her journey home at a brisk pace. She wanted nothing more than to be safe inside her house.

The cold hand that clamped over her mouth sent shivers down her spine, and the arm that grabbed her by the neck almost strangled her. She was being pulled backwards. She tried to look around, but her assailant had such a firm grip on her neck that she couldn't turn her head. Was this the creepy old man, had he come back to kill her? If so, he was surprisingly strong for his age and stature. She tried to scream, but only a muffled murmur came out through her attacker's hand. She was dragged through bushes and dumped unceremoniously on the ground, face up; she then saw her attacker for the first time.

It was a woman, no taller than Sarah but quite a bit older, perhaps in her mid-fifties. She wore a mismatched outfit of a red t-shirt and a long, green skirt. Most strikingly, her skin glowed blue.

Sarah screamed.

New Girl

"There's no-one around to hear you, love," chided the woman, "You'll meet your death here."

"What are you?" gasped Sarah.

"Your worst nightmare," said her assailant, her face twisted into a grim and insane smile as she leaned forwards over Sarah.

Sarah looked around desperately; she was in an overgrown field dotted with rocks. No, not rocks; tombstones. This was an old graveyard. All around, there were clumps of freshly-dug earth. Had this woman risen from the ground? Had that crazy old man been telling the truth?

She grabbed a chunk of earth and threw it in her attacker's eyes. The woman stopped in her tracks, and Sarah used the momentary confusion to scramble to her feet and begin to run.

New Girl

She hopped back through the bushes and onto the main road, but she was quickly followed. She began to run in the direction of her home, hoping the zombie's years of rest underground had lowered her fitness levels.

She could hear the creature's footsteps gaining on her fast. She was going to be caught. She was going to die. It was all over.

A glint of steel caught her eye; something was embedded in a tree at the side of the road. No; two somethings. The hilts of two swords stuck out of a tree about ten metres in front of her.

The man had mentioned swords. Maybe these things were her only hope. She had no idea how to use a sword, though, and they looked pretty deeply embedded in the tree. Would she be able to get them out in time? She didn't have much option but to try.

New Girl

As soon as she reached the tree she grasped the hilt of one of the swords with her two hands and pulled with all her might. To her surprise, it came so easily she fell backwards onto the road, still holding the sword. It was light as a feather. She looked to her right; the zombie was only a few metres away from her. Springing to her feet with an athleticism she had never known in herself before, Sarah brandished the sword. Swordsmanship came easily, it seemed natural, and there was a glint of fear in the zombie's eyes as she stopped dead not far from Sarah.

Sarah sprang forward and jabbed the sword into the zombie's chest. The zombie gasped and fell back, but then lunged for Sarah, who light-footedly circumvented the attack. What was going on? Where had these new skills come from?

She hurriedly pulled the other sword from the tree and, wielding one in each hand, sprang forward. In the parry that followed, she managed to chop off the creature's arm, which instantly turned to skeletal bone. The zombie fell back, wailing, and Sarah ran for her life.

It wasn't long before she began to hear footsteps behind her; she looked around and saw that the one-armed zombie was following her. Clearly, the loss of a limb was no deterrent to these creatures. Was there any way of killing them? Did the fact that they were already dead prevent them from being killed? And, most importantly, how many were there? From the way the old man had talked, it had sounded as though there would be a whole army of them. Were the others lying in wait, waiting to see what this sole zombie made of Sarah? Why Sarah? Why did she have to be the one fighting zombies? It was her first day at school; she had been hoping to maybe make some friends, do well in her classes. She hadn't asked for a destiny.

She cursed her unfamiliarity with the area as she ran. She knew she was close to her house, but she wasn't entirely sure what lay between there and her present location. She wished she knew of some kind of hiding place.

Feeling as though she would probably fight better with just one sword, she threw one into the ditch on her right and shifted the other one to her right hand. It was time to face the zombie. She turned around, stepped to the side, stuck out her leg and tripped up the still-running zombie, who fell face-down on the ground. She took the opportunity to slash at the zombie's leg and, to her surprise, she managed to cut off its foot.

Now that her enemy had been considerably slowed down, Sarah felt as though she were more in a position to make a getaway. She leapt over a hedge and ran through a field, down a hill,

New Girl

under a hedge and into another field,
and dove into a patch of thick gorse.
She lay still, trying to catch her breath.

What on earth had just happened?

Chapter 5

She stayed in the gorse for well over an hour, lying down uncomfortably with her schoolbag still on her back and the remaining sword still in her right hand. She could make very little sense of the events of the afternoon, but she was fairly certain that the danger had passed; the zombie hadn't followed her here. Aside from the birdsong, everything was silent. She wasn't near a road, not that it would matter as a passing car around these parts was a momentous event. It would begin to darken soon enough, and she needed to get home. She didn't know where she was. She would have to try her best to retrace her footsteps and hope not to encounter any zombies on the way.

Zombies. Zombies were real. She was planning her route home around zombies. She shook her head at the ridiculousness of it all.

She examined the sword; it looked old, but freshly polished. Some strange, foreign writing was inscribed on the hilt, and the blade itself was scratched as though it had seen much use. She wondered who had last held this sword.

Sword in hand, she stood up and set off back the way she had come, noting that her arms and legs were all scratched from the time spent leaping through bushes. She would certainly be covering up more for school tomorrow. She struggled to walk in the stilettos, and she was quite impressed with herself that she had managed to escape a zombie in them. If this was to be her destiny, she would have to invest in more sensible shoes.

New Girl

How could she be destined to kill zombies? How could zombies be real? Why was this happening to her?

She managed to retrace her steps with surprising ease, and she soon found herself back at the place where she had cut off the zombie's foot; a small pile of human bones sat on the road, but other than that there was no sign of any strange activity. She trudged up the road, arriving at the laneway that led to her house within minutes. She dumped the sword in the nearest hedge, fixed her hair as best as she could, brushed the remaining leaves and twigs off her clothes, took a deep breath and made her way towards her front door.

As soon as she began to turn the key she heard footsteps, and she opened the door to see her mother standing right there.

New Girl

"Sarah!" she shrieked, "Where have you been?"

"Sorry," Sarah said, "I got held up."

"Held up? HELD UP? You choose the day when dead bodies are found in your school to get held up? And what happened to your legs? What have you been doing?"

Sarah said nothing and walked past her mother.

"Come back here, young lady!"

Sarah ignored her mother's remonstrations, exited the kitchen slamming the door behind her and went up the stairs to her new bedroom. She locked the door behind her and lay down on the bed, tears coming unbidden to her eyes. She had expected a fresh start in a new place to be difficult, but nothing like this. How could zombies exist? How could she be destined to fight them? Why couldn't

she at least have had a week or two to
settle into her new school before this
had happened?

She ignored her mother's calls for dinner
that night, lying instead on her bed. She
presumed Dónal and Liz wouldn't be
going to the pub; the whole community
would be in mourning.

She thought back to the dishevelled old
man, the man who had warned her
about this, who had told her she needed
to find the swords. What was his role in
all this? It seemed as though he was on
her side, although he wasn't exactly
being particularly free with whatever
information he had. How could she find
him again? Or would he find her? And
just who was he, and what connection
did he have to these zombies, these
'Awakened', as he had called them? She
idly wondered if the zombies knew
where she lived, and she then resolved to
stop thinking those sort of thoughts.

New Girl

She would worry herself sick. Besides, if they did know where she lived, they would of course come and kill her in her sleep and there would be nothing she could do about it, so worrying was entirely pointless. She wondered if she would become one of them if they killed her, but then she remembered that she had resolved to stop thinking. The problem was, the more she tried not to think the more she thought.

She needed to use the bathroom, but she didn't want to risk having to talk to either of her parents, so she held it in until long after she had heard the sounds of them both going to bed. Once she had used the bathroom, she returned to her room, took off her thin layer of make-up and got into her pyjamas. She curled up in bed, cuddling her tattered teddy bear, hoping to wake up the next day and find that this had all been a bad dream.

New Girl

She was running through unfamiliar
fields, chased by an army of zombies.
There were at least a hundred of them,
and they all glowed blue. The sun shone
bright in the sky; it was a clear, cloudless
day with no sign of any recent rain. Up
ahead of her, Sarah could see an old,
decrepit farmhouse; perhaps she could
take refuge there. She ran towards it,
hoping she would reach it in time. She
didn't have either of the swords; hiding
was her only hope. The house loomed
closer and closer until finally she was at
the door.

The door opened from the inside and
more zombies spilled out. She turned
around; the ones chasing her had caught
up. She was trapped. She pushed her way
through the throng, feeling cold hands
grabbing her as she went. She had to get
away. She had to find the swords.

She found herself facing the old man.
The zombies had disappeared.

New Girl

"I tried to warn you," he said, "but you didn't listen."

The man was grabbed from behind by a female zombie, who broke his neck in one swift movement, allowing him to drop to the ground before she started towards Sarah, her face twisted into a menacing grin.

"Sarah Reilly, Killer of the Undead," she hissed, "Do you know who I am? Do you know how much you should fear me?"

The creature laughed as she advanced on Sarah, who stood rooted to the spot. She was going to be killed. This was it; this was the end.

Sarah woke up in a cold sweat, breathing heavily, fervently hoping her eerily vivid dream had not been in any way prophetic. She checked her clock; 6am. She might as well get up. At least it was

New Girl

Friday; she would have two days with no school ahead of her by the time today was over.

The house was quiet, and she crept downstairs softly, hoping not to wake either of her parents. Maybe she could even leave the house before they got up. When she went into the kitchen, however, the light was already on and her dad was sitting at the table in his dressing gown, supping on a mug of coffee.

"Morning," he said, "Ready to talk to your dear old parents?"

Sarah grimaced.

"Sorry," she said, "I had a rough day yesterday."

"Not a nice first day," said her dad.

New Girl

He was talking about the murder. He didn't know what had really happened. He didn't know that Sarah's life seemed to have changed direction forever.

"Dad?" she asked, "Can I have a lift to school today?"

He looked at his watch.

"If you're okay with being an hour early, yeah, sure," he said.

"Thanks," she said, feeling quite relieved as she put some bread in the toaster and put the kettle on for a mug of tea, "How was your first day at work?"

"Interesting," he said, "Half of these new employees barely know how to turn on a computer. It'll take some time to get things up and running."

Sarah's dad had some important job in a computer firm that had recently opened a factory just outside of Ballynavolan, and he had been asked to move to

New Girl

Meath and head up the factory; Sarah had begged him not to take the job, to stay in Dublin, but she gathered there was a large amount of money involved.

If he hadn't taken the job, Sarah mused, this never would have happened. She wouldn't have been given a destiny. But maybe this had always been her destiny, maybe her father getting that job and deciding to take it had been part of some higher plan.

Or maybe she had just been in the wrong place at the wrong time. Maybe that man had entered the school grounds with the aim of anointing the first teenager he found. Why couldn't it have been the boy who was cutting class to smoke? She hadn't done anything wrong; all she had done was got lost and now she was being punished for it. The words 'destiny' and 'fate' sounded awfully noble, but it appeared that this particular destiny came with a high

amount of personal risk attached to it.
Why couldn't she have had a destiny that
didn't involve any fighting? Why couldn't
she have just not had a destiny at all?
What would happen now? Would she
have to spend all her time running from
the zombies? Would that man re-appear
and teach her how to fight them? Or
would she die at their hands in the next
few days?

She thought back to the man; he had
had a strange accent. She thought
perhaps it might have been Australian;
she had never met anyone from
Australia, but she had heard the accent
on television. Were there zombies in
Australia, too? Was that where they came
from? Had they only recently come to
Ireland? How did they get here? She had
a sudden mental image of blue-glowing
zombies sitting in rows of seats on a
long-haul aircraft, sipping apéritifs while
reading newspapers.

New Girl

Sarah had too many questions and nobody to answer them. She sighed as she drank her mug of tea; life was now horrendously complicated, and she felt as though she were drowning in some kind of awfully unfamiliar sea.

Chapter 6

They left the house at twenty past seven, Sarah wearing black jeans and a red-and-yellow floral blouse along with the most comfortable pair of flat shoes she owned. Father and daughter passed the journey to school in silence; he dropped her off at the gates, and she exited the car without even bothering to say goodbye. She didn't feel like saying anything. She missed their old house, she missed her old school and her friends, and most of all she missed the sense of normalcy that went hand in hand with not being destined to fight the undead. She suddenly remembered that she had been supposed to ring Niamh, her best friend from Dublin, the previous night, but in all the hubbub it had slipped her mind. She didn't feel like talking to Niamh anyway; she wouldn't be able to tell her what was really going on, and she hated the thought of lying to her best friend. Niamh probably hadn't even noticed the forgotten phone call anyway; she had other friends, other things in her life, and she would probably be busy with school. Sarah tried to remember what it was like to have worries more mundane than whether or not the undead would manage to kill her today; she realised that, even though this time yesterday she hadn't known of the zombies' existence, she couldn't remember what it was like to feel safe, what it was like to feel as though she knew the terms and conditions of the world she inhabited.

Once her dad had driven away, she lingered outside the gates for a while, hoping the man who had warned her about the zombies might be around, but she was to be disappointed; eventually, more students began to arrive, some by car and others on foot, and Sarah gave up searching for the elusive stranger and went into the grounds, looking around for familiar faces. She couldn't see anyone she recognised as being in her year, although she was certain she had already forgotten some of the faces she had encountered yesterday. She was relieved to see that she had done a better job of dressing to blend in today, and she no longer felt as though everyone's eyes were on her.

She jumped around as she felt a hand on her shoulder; it was Liz, wearing black leggings and an oversized violently pink shirt, her dark brown curls dangling freely down her back.

"Jesus," said Sarah, "You scared me half to death."

"Sorry," said Liz, grimacing, "How are you doing?"

For a split-second, Sarah thought of telling Liz the truth, of pulling her aside and telling her that zombies were real, that the undead were threatening to kill

New Girl

them all, but then she realised how ludicrous it all sounded.

"Fine," she lied, "What have we got first thing today?"

"Irish," said Liz pulling a face, "With Ms Murphy, the woman with the most irritating voice in the world."

Sarah laughed.

"Come on," said Liz, "If we get there early we can sit at the back, and she's incredibly short-sighted. She never asks the people at the back anything because she's not really too sure who they are."

Sarah managed a smile as she walked through the school gates alongside her new friend. She could forget about zombies for now. She looked around; already, the campus seemed more like home, more familiar, less threatening.

She then caught sight of a stain on the ground; it was at the place where the man had anointed her, a splash of the strange-smelling shimmering liquid. A shiver went down her spine. There was no escaping this destiny of hers.

Sarah payed scant attention during Irish, unable to take her mind off the previous day's events. Liz had been right about Ms Murphy; she completely ignored the back two rows of her class, and thus Sarah was safe from having to answer any questions, which was fortunate because she was unable to think of anything other than the undead.

She needed to find that man again. She needed answers. She needed help. She needed to know what the hell she was supposed to do. She needed someone with whom she could split this enormous burden, and she had a feeling that strange old man was the only person who could help her with that. She imagined what Liz or Dónal or either of her parents or Niamh would

say if she told them what was going on;
they would think her quite mad and
would probably drag her straight to a
doctor.

After Irish, she told Liz and Dónal, who
had been unfortunate enough to be last
to arrive and thus bear the brunt of Ms
Murphy's questioning, that she would be
along to maths in a second, that she just
had to go to the bathroom.

She walked straight past the bathroom
and out the door into the quadrangle.
Looking around, she saw that there were
enough students to-ing and fro-ing that
she would be able to get out unnoticed.
She purposefully made her way towards
the open front gate and slipped out,
ready to find out who she really was,
ready to find out how she could best
these zombies.

"Sarah Reilly!"

New Girl

She spun around, hoping to see the man she sought; she groaned inwardly when she realised it was Mr Keegan.

"Where are you going, Sarah?" he asked sternly.

"I just, uh, I needed some fresh air," she said, "I've come over all faint."

"Fresh air?" he asked, his eyebrows raised, "You couldn't get that within the school gates?"

"I, uh, no. I couldn't. I'm claustrophobic," said Sarah, clutching at straws.

"Nice try," said Mr Keegan, "Come on, back inside."

Grudgingly, Sarah re-entered the school gates and made her way into the building where she was supposed to be. She looked around; Mr Keegan was still watching her intently from outside, a warning look on his stern, pointed face.

New Girl

She ducked into the bathroom, unsure of how she was going to proceed.

The bathroom was mercifully empty, and Sarah took several deep breaths. Did Mr Keegan constantly patrol the school gates? She imagined not; surely he must have other, more important things to do. She would wait ten minutes and then try again. This was important, she couldn't let Keegan stop her. He didn't understand what was at stake.

She paced back and forth for what seemed like forever, periodically checking the time on the phone. At last, the ten minutes she had promised herself were up, and she slipped back out into the now-empty corridor.

She walked softly towards the end of the building and out the door; looking around, she saw that the place was deserted save for a lone figure standing at the far end of the campus. He looked too young to be a staff member, but slightly too old to be a student, and Sarah's heart began to beat faster as he spotted her and began to head quite quickly in her direction. Maybe he was a teacher. Or maybe he was in league with the zombies. Either way, she didn't want to find out. Taking a deep breath and resolving not to look back, she walked briskly towards the gates, exited and started down the road, fervently hoping the man would not follow her. She had had quite enough of strange men over the last day. Why her? What was so special about her? Why did she have to have a destiny? She wasn't even athletic, or skilled at fighting, although she had to admit that she had done quite a good job when she had had the swords in her hands. Maybe she was only competent with the swords. Then again, maybe it was the swords that were doing all the work. If that was the case, why couldn't someone else have her destiny? Why did it have to be her? She didn't seem to be bringing any special skills to the role; in fact, she had absolutely no idea what she was doing or how she was supposed to go about it.

All in all, it seemed as though destiny had got it wrong.

Chapter 7

She swiftly beheaded the Awakened woman who lay writhing on the road; with only two complete limbs, she would neither blend in nor make a good fighter. Picking up the bones, she hurled them into a nearby ditch, leaving just the bones of the detached foot. Perhaps that would scare the child.

She was disgruntled that Nam had managed to follow her here so easily, but there was nothing she could do about it now. She had hoped to get a head start before he had a chance to call a young girl, but at least now she had seen the child fight, and she had some idea of her weaknesses.

It would be time to move on soon, but it troubled her that no clear leader was emerging from the group of dead she had raised. Perhaps she would need to hold some sort of contest, some test of their abilities, at least to see who among them had the enthusiasm and the drive to succeed, if nothing else.

She ran back to the ditch, not wishing to be seen whilst she glowed blue, and then trudged through the empty fields to her newly-acquisitioned farmhouse. She would have to decide today what to do; she needed to move on to the next town first thing in the morning. She would come back to Ballynavolan, of course, but she would need to set things in motion throughout this island. She would avoid Dublin for now, as she would risk drawing attention to herself and to her people, but she would stir up as many graveyards as she could throughout the sparsely-populated countryside.

Of course, she hadn't expected a Killer of the Undead to be called so soon, but she would swiftly sort out the girl. She hoped to be able to track Nam down, but he had always proven elusive; he knew how to hide himself. Her goal with Nam had always been to trap him rather than kill him; if he died, his powers would pass to his heir, but if he was locked away somewhere no-one would be able to bestow powers on these girls and she could kill them off one by one. Of course, that was what the Sleepers had been trying to do for millennia, and it was a near impossible feat.

She knew something was wrong as soon as she saw the door of her farmhouse; it was open, swinging back and forth in the wind. What had happened? Had some of her army escaped? She had taken the key, and she didn't think there were any likely dissenters among them; in fact, they had all seemed quite apathetic. She broke into a run and didn't stop until she was inside the house.

The kitchen was empty.

Her army had fled.

Cursing her inattentiveness, she searched every room on the lower floor, hoping at least some had remained. She found none, and went upstairs.

New Girl

Nothing like this had ever happened before; clearly, she had awakened something not entirely human. She knew they had not been massacred; there were no bones, and it would have taken someone a long time to clear away that many.

She entered a bedroom on the upper floor, and jumped as she heard the door close behind her. One of the men she had awakened stood at the door, a menacing grin on his face.

"Sleeper," he hissed.

"What have you done?" she asked.

"I've taken control of your band of merry men," he said, "and I'm here to take over from you."

He lifted a sword which she hadn't seen until now.

"Wait!" she yelled, "You won't be the new Sleeper."

New Girl

"Yes I will," he said, "I was the fifth-last you awakened. I've slain the other four."

The Sleeper opened her mouth to speak, but she found no words. She ran towards the window and tried to open it; it was too stiff. The man was gaining on her. She ran back to the door and, to her surprise and relief, it opened. She scurried down the stairs, into the kitchen and out the front door, running across the field, knowing that the next few moments would decide her fate.

The moment she tripped over the stone, she knew she was dead. She made one last effort to scramble to her feet, but then she felt the blade at her neck, and then she was gone.

Chapter 8

As the school was on a country road some distance from the town, Sarah saw no-one other than the primary school children playing on their breaktime as she passed their yard. She thought again of the three young children of the deceased couple and wondered what would happen to them.

She shook herself; there was no time to think of that now. She would retrace her steps of the day before, go back to where she had encountered the man. She kept her head down as she walked, ignoring the three cars that passed, hoping she wouldn't be recognised as a truant from the local school. She had urgent business, something far more important than maths or chemistry.

The journey was a lot easier in the flat shoes she was wearing today than it had

New Girl

been yesterday, and she found herself making good time. She didn't really care that she was missing classes; she knew her absence would be noted, but this was a matter of life or death. She needed to know how to deal with these blue-glowing creatures. She needed to be able to protect herself. She needed help. She needed answers.

She passed Dónal and Liz's houses and continued down the road until she reached the spot where the man had confronted her. She didn't know what she was expecting, and now that she was here the whole venture seemed silly. Why would that man be waiting here for her? She peered into the bushes, not really knowing why, and then concluded she had been foolish to ever come here. She would go back to school; hopefully she wouldn't have missed too much and wouldn't get in too much trouble.

New Girl

The blue-glowing creature who stood in her path when she turned around, however, didn't seem to have any intention of letting her get by him.

She turned on her heel and ran, trying to remember where she had discarded that oh-so-useful sword the previous day. She knew it wasn't far from that bend in the road up ahead. Just a bit further, then she would have it.

She plunged into the bushes, and was relieved to find that she was in almost the right place; edging forward, she picked up the sword.

The zombie jumped onto her back, and Sarah screamed and howled with pain as it sank its teeth into her neck.

Summoning all her strength and gripping the sword tightly, Sarah rolled over. The creature was thrown off her, and she scrambled to her feet, brandishing the sword wildly. She wasn't too sure what the best course of action was, but she was fairly certain that it would be pertinent to chop off some of his limbs, just as she had done with that previous zombie. She tried to do an awkward sort of leap forward in the hope of jabbing his arm, but he lunged for her at the same time and knocked her to the ground, flinging the sword out of her hand.

She scrambled across the ground and grabbed the sword, but the zombie kicked her roughly across the grass; he was strong, there was no doubt about that.

"What do you want from me?" she called to him.

"To kill you," he sneered, "To kill your kind, to kill your mentor, and to take over this whole town."

"My... mentor?" she asked.

New Girl

"Don't play stupid with me, girl," he hissed, "I know you're a Killer of the Undead."

Sarah didn't know what to make of this, although the words 'Killer of the Undead' seemed vaguely familiar for some reason, so she got to her feet, grabbed the sword again and scurried backwards, hoping to at least put some distance between her and this thing while she tried to figure out what to do.

She had already established that cutting off a part of a zombie turned it to bone. What if she managed to cut the entire creature in half at the torso? His waist and legs would be gone, and he certainly wouldn't be able to run after her.

Taking a deep breath, she lunged forward; catching the zombie completely by surprise she ran the blade through his midriff. His bottom half fell off almost comically and turned to bone, and his top half fell to the ground where it was left writhing.

Sarah ran.

Once back on the main road, she decided the best course of action would be to return to school. No zombie had tried to attack her there; maybe she would be relatively safe. She began to walk briskly back up the road, back towards school.

She suddenly realised that there was a man coming towards her. Was it another zombie? She gripped her sword in readiness as it approached.

It wasn't a zombie.

It was Dónal.

New Girl

Hastily, Sarah tossed the sword into the nearest ditch and tried to appear nonchalant.

"Well, well, well," called Dónal as he approached, "Here's our truant."

Sarah blushed.

"What are you doing here?" she asked.

"I could ask you the same question. Come on, where are you headed?"

"Back to school," said Sarah.

"What, you skipped school so you could go back there?"

"I-" began Sarah, and then realised she really had nothing to say.

"You what?"

"I had to… I had to do something."

Dónal raised his eyebrows.

New Girl

"You're a very mysterious girl," he commented, "Is this what all Dublin girls are like, or is it just you?"

Sarah said nothing.

"Come on," said Dónal, "Let's go back."

They walked silently for a while, Sarah feeling slightly comforted by having someone else there, even if Dónal probably wouldn't be all that much use in a fight.

"Where were you going?" she asked him at length.

He shrugged.

"I was looking for you. I wanted to see if you were okay. Dangerous times around here, Sarah. Dangerous times."

She wondered whether he was genuinely concerned or just nosey; she contemplated asking him, but then decided it would be unwise to add fuel to the fire. She still didn't know him all that well. Besides, she felt a little safer now that she wasn't alone, and for that she was grateful.

It was only ten minutes from lunchtime by the time they got back to the school, and they lingered outside the gates until at last they saw students begin to spill out of the buildings; they then mingled with the crowd and went to the bench where they had sat the previous day. They were joined not long after by Liz.

"Where the hell were the two of you?" she asked, hurt evident in her voice, "You left me alone!"

Sarah looked at Dónal, and Dónal looked at Sarah.

New Girl

"We just went for a wander," said Dónal, winking at Sarah, "Thought I'd show her the sights. How was everything here?"

Liz didn't answer, instead giving Dónal a thunderous glare. All three sat down and began to eat their lunch in silence.

"Keegan wants everyone in the school to see the chaplain," Liz said at length, "because of the Joyces. We'll all be called in the afternoon."

"What's the chaplain like?" asked Sarah.

Liz grimaced.

"Nun," she said.

"Is she nice?" asked Sarah.

Liz shrugged.

"She's a nun."

"Liz hates nuns," explained Dónal.

New Girl

"They freak me out," Liz said plaintively.

"She's not too bad," said Dónal, "But, sure, you won't have to see her anyway, I'd imagine."

"True," said Sarah, musing that she more than anyone needed someone to talk to right now. Of course, she certainly couldn't tell a nun that she was being attacked by zombies. She didn't know who she could tell. She needed to track down that strange man.

Sarah and Dónal had chemistry after lunch, while Liz went to geography.

"Please please please be my lab partner," said Dónal, "Mrs Ryan pairs us up if we haven't decided by the start of the first class. I'll write up the experiments for both of us if you do all the actual work."

New Girl

"Deal," said Sarah, and the two of them took a bench at the back of the lab.

They were a class of only eight, and Mrs Ryan bade the two pairs who had sat at the back move forward until they were all gathered in the front two rows. She wasn't long into her explanation of what they would be doing when Dónal was called to see the chaplain, and so Sarah was left to do the experiment on her own. She didn't mind; she liked working on her own, and it would give her some time to think on her predicament.

It soon became apparent, however, that no amount of thought she could give the matter would amount to a solution. She had to talk to the man; he was her only hope. What if the zombies had already killed him? No, she couldn't think like that. Besides, he seemed to know what he was doing, so surely if she could stay alive this long so could he.

New Girl

She thought back to the other strange man, the younger one she had seen earlier in the school grounds. Who was he? Was he involved in all this? She wished Liz or Dónal had been there when she had seen him so she could have asked if he was someone local, if they recognised him. Maybe he had nothing to do with all this, maybe he had just happened to be standing there while Sarah was leaving. Still, though, he had begun to approach her. It was probably safest to assume that he did have some involvement in this whole thing.

The bell rang and Sarah packed up her things, barely listening to the chatter of the others in her class. She made her way through the school and down into the basement for French.

She hadn't had time to go over anything since yesterday, and it was with a certain amount of trepidation that she entered the classroom. She was, however, very

New Girl

relieved to see that Ms Bell was not there; instead, an elderly man with whispy, white hair was taking the class.

"Where's Ms Bell?" she whispered, sitting down beside Lorna, the blonde with the orange face.

"Out sick," said Lorna, "We've got a free period."

Sarah smiled to herself. Finally, things were looking up.

She made a start on her chemistry homework, but she was finding it very difficult to concentrate and she soon found herself thinking about zombies once more. Had they all come from that dug-up old graveyard? Would more rise? What about the couple who had been killed, would they rise, too? How did this whole thing work; could any dead person be resurrected as a zombie?

New Girl

The bell rang, sooner than she had thought it would, and she made her way up to her form room for English. She now knew that the overly-jolly year head and English teacher was named Mrs McCluskey, and she also knew that she was one of the most detested teachers in the school; jolly on the outside, she held a bitter streak on the inside and was not above enjoying making her students cry. As soon as Sarah walked into the classroom she saw Liz beckoning to her from a double desk in the middle; she went to join her.

"We're going to McKenna's tonight," Liz whispered once Sarah had sat down, "Coming?"

"Sure," whispered Sarah.

"Cool," said Liz, "Meet us there at seven."

New Girl

"Quiet, boys and girls!" yelled Mrs McCluskey's shrill voice, "Settle down, settle down!"

Sarah tried her best to make herself invisible as her first English class in Ballynavolan Community School began; unfortunately, she didn't succeed. She was the first person the shrill old woman selected to answer a question, and all thought of zombies soon left her mind; Mrs McCluskey, as it turned out, was just as frightening as any of the living dead. At least, Sarah mused, she didn't bite; not literally, anyway.

Chapter 9

The walk home was less morose than the previous day's had been, and the three chatted amiably, mainly analysing the various snide comments Mrs McCluskey had directed towards her pupils during English.

"That woman has to be close to retirement," said Dónal bitterly, "The sooner she goes, the better."

"I dunno," said Liz, "I reckon she's younger than she looks. I'd say we'll be stuck with her until we're finished."

"Maybe we're looking at this the wrong way," suggested Sarah, "It's character-building. Dealing with her, I mean. Once we've put up with her we'll be able to put up with anything. It's almost like she's preparing us for the real world, in a weird sort of way."

New Girl

The other two paused for thought.

"No," they said simultaneously at last.

"There's no good way of looking at this," said Dónal, "That woman is a demon, a hell-beast, pure and simple."

Sarah said nothing. Knowing what a real hell-beast was like, she'd rather deal with Mrs McCluskey any day.

At length, they reached Drumoolly; Sarah could just make out the chimneys of the four farmhouses of the townland beyond the tall trees that separated the farms from the road. Dónal and Liz would leave here, and Sarah would be alone, vulnerable, helpless. Come to think of it, she was just as vulnerable and helpless with them, but something about having company made her feel a little safer. Maybe it was the distraction of their conversation; it took her mind off the zombies. In order to fear

104

something, she had to be thinking about it.

"See you tomorrow, Sarah," said Liz.

"Bye," she called to the two of them, trying to stem the wobble in her voice. She had to be brave.

She didn't see Liz and Dónal double back and furtively begin to follow her as she continued down the road towards her house.

Sarah peered around carefully at the road ahead of her as she walked, hoping to see some sign of the strange man and fervently hoping there would be no zombies about. She idly wondered what had happened to the one she had chopped in half earlier.

She nipped into the hedge where she had discarded the sword; she wanted to be prepared lest she be set upon. It was still there. She picked it up and felt that sudden surge of knowledge, of power. Somehow, when she held the sword, she knew how to be a fighter. Grasping the hilt with both hands, she returned to the road. She felt different, more aware of her surroundings, more capable of taking care of herself. Still, she had no desire to engage in a fight; she still fervently hoped there would be no zombies around.

She kept her eyes peeled as she walked down the road, and a pile of rocks at the side of the road caught her eye; there was a piece of A4 paper trying to escape from under it. She approached it and knelt down, taking away the rocks and grasping the fluttering page.

"MEET ME IN GRAVEYARD. WE HAVE MUCH TO DISCUSS. YOU ARE IN GRAVE DANGER."

New Girl

This must be from the mysterious man! Excitedly, she stood up and studied the map drawn below the message; it appeared the graveyard in question was not the old one she had been to previously but was another one just a little way past her house. She continued on down the road, scrutinising the roughly-drawn map as she walked. Finally, she would get some answers! She wondered why the man hadn't waited for her himself at the side of the road; maybe there was something that needed to be done in the graveyard. Maybe he was killing zombies.

She passed the laneway that led to her house and continued on; she would need to turn right up here. She made the turn and found herself facing the open iron-wrought gates of a small graveyard surrounded by a low stone wall.

She walked in; the cemetery looked frequently-visited, although there was

107

New Girl

no-one there at the moment. There were about two dozen graves, almost all richly decorated with fresh flowers, and three large mausoleums towards the back which looked far older than any of the other graves.

Sarah walked forwards cautiously; she couldn't see the man she sought anywhere. Maybe he was hiding; maybe he didn't want to draw any attention to himself until she had arrived. She scrutinised every inch of the cemetery but saw no sign that anyone was around, and she felt certain the man was too wide to hide himself behind the low wall of the graveyard. What was going on? Why would he have left her a note if he hadn't intended to be here?

Then she saw them; the zombies. There were four of them, emerging from behind the mausoleums, walking slowly towards her, malevolent grins etched on their blue faces.

New Girl

"We see you got our note," said one, and the other three laughed.

It was a trap.

Sarah turned around and ran straight into Liz.

"Run!" yelled Sarah.

"What's going on?" asked Liz.

"Just run!"

The two ran out the gates of the graveyard and encountered Dónal, who was sitting calmly at the side of the road.

"What-?" he began, jumping awkwardly to his feet.

"Follow me!" called Sarah, and Liz and Dónal did so.

She wished she had some idea of where she was going as she led her two new friends to what could very well be their deaths. She jumped over a hedge and into a ditch, awkwardly holding the sword ahead of her, and the others followed; she motioned to them to lay low.

"Where did they go?" she heard one of the zombies say above them.

"Didn't see," said another gruffly, "They must've gone over the hedge. Split up, you two take that side, we'll take this one."

Sarah stood up in the ditch, gripping the sword tightly, waiting.

The zombies never came. Perhaps they were in a different part of the hedge. Sarah had an idea.

"Come on," she whispered, "We'll go back to the graveyard."

They crept through the ditch and down a perpendicular ditch through which a

New Girl

trickling stream of water flowed, coming out behind the graveyard; they climbed over a short stone wall and were inside. There were no zombies visible.

"In there," whispered Sarah, pointing towards a back entrance to one of the mausoleums. Liz and Dónal cautiously went in, and she followed, closing the door behind her and taking her phone out of her pocket to illuminate the area. Thick layers of dust lay over raised stone graves; no-one had been in here in a long time. She could taste the dust in her mouth; this wasn't a particularly pleasant place to hide.

"Sarah," hissed Liz, "What the hell is going on?"

Sarah took a deep breath.

"Zombies," she whispered simply.

New Girl

"Zombies?" asked Liz in an incredulous whisper, "Is this what you do in Dublin for fun?"

"No!" protested Sarah as quietly as possible, "This only started when I came here. Remember that man I told you about? The man who soaked me with water at school? He was going on about zombies, and then - zombies. They appeared. They attacked me. They keep attacking me, and they're blue, and I don't know what to do, except for some reason I have these two swords and they're the only things that seem to do anything to them."

"Two swords?" asked Dónal with interest, "Where's the other one?"

"In the hedge outside my house," said Sarah, "I couldn't exactly turn up at home with a sword, could I?"

"So the man gave you the swords?"

New Girl

"No, he told me to find the swords. I don't know why he didn't just give them to me, anyone could've come along and taken them."

"Okay," said Liz, "So zombies are real. Do they eat brains?"

"I don't know," said Sarah, "One of them bit my neck, maybe he was trying to get at my brain."

"It bit your neck?" asked Dónal, his expression one of disgust, "Doesn't that mean you're a zombie now?"

"I think that's vampires," said Liz.

"Shut up, both of you!" whispered Sarah, "We have a serious problem!"

"This is totally freaky," said Dónal.

"Actually," said Liz, "I think it's kind of cool."

New Girl

"Cool?" asked Sarah, *"Cool?* We're about to be killed and you think it's cool?"

Liz shrugged.

"It's an exciting way to go. Besides, we're not going to be killed, because you seem to be some kind of superhero with a sword."

"I'm not a superhero!" hissed Sarah, "I'm just someone who got caught up in the middle of all of this!"

"Sorry, love," said Dónal, "I think it's pretty clear you're a superhero now."

"Look," said Sarah, "I just want to get out of this stupid crypt, preferably alive. Any ideas?"

The other two shook their heads.

"Great," muttered Sarah, "Do I have to do everything?"

Liz shrugged.

New Girl

"You're the superhero."

Sarah paced up and down the crypt, trying to figure out what to do. It was only a matter of time before the zombies would find them; there were only so many ways Sarah and the others could have gone. What if the creatures were outside the mausoleum right now? What if there were more than four? What if they went away and came back with some of their friends? Most importantly, just how many were there in total? Would they keep on coming, would each one she felled be instantly replaced? She cursed herself for being so stupid as to fall for that note; in her naïvety it hadn't occurred to her that zombies could do something so seemingly human as scribble a note and leave it for her to find. She reminded herself that these were the risen dead, that they had been human once, that they knew what humans did, how humans thought.

She closely examined the doors at either end of the crypt, trying to see if there were any gaps that would allow her to see out, but she had no luck. There were cross-shaped holes etched into the side walls of the structure, but these were much too high for her to see out of them. She began to pace up and down again, hoping some brilliant idea would come to her.

There was a loud bang at the back door, and it swung open loudly. Blue-glowing zombies began to pile in, moving swiftly towards the three terrified teenagers. There were certainly more than four; Sarah could see at least eight, and she felt sure there were more behind those. They seemed crazed, desperate, almost as though they needed to shed blood more than they needed anything else in the world.

New Girl

"The other door!" yelled Liz.

Sarah ran, pushed open the door with all her might and burst out into the middle of another trio of zombies. Brandishing the sword, she pushed through, dragging Dónal with her by the wrist; she could see Liz following. She began to run, Dónal and Liz behind her, the zombies behind them.

Chapter 10

Sarah had had to do an awful lot of running over the past few days, and she was beginning to get more than a little sick of it. Her thighs ached, and she longed to sit down without fear of being chased, to curl up on the sofa in her living room with a cup of tea and some semblance of peace of mind. She wanted to go back to normal, to go back to the way things had been two days ago.

But she couldn't. Right now, all she could do was try to survive. That, and make sure her new friends survived. If only it was as simple as it all sounded.

A blue-glowing woman jumped out in front of her; Sarah aimed for her face with the sword, but the zombie ducked out of the way, grabbed Sarah's arm and flipped her over. The sword flew out of her hand as she fell, and she hit the ground face-down with considerable force.

By the time she had scrambled to her feet, her ears now ringing, there were zombies everywhere; the sword was several metres away from her, over beside Liz. All three teenagers were unarmed and, though the zombies had no weapons, their brute strength was a formidable weapon in itself, far more than any sword or mace could have been. Sarah felt naked without the sword; without it, she was just another teenage girl. She was too far away to reach it; two snarling, grimacing zombies stood between her and the place where it lay.

"Pick up the sword!" Sarah screamed at Liz. Liz went to grab it, but couldn't seem to pick it up.

"What's going on?" yelled Sarah.

New Girl

"It's too heavy!" called Liz as she tugged at the hilt, "It won't budge!"

"What are you on about?" screeched Sarah as the zombies moved towards them, "It's light as a feather!" Despite her words, Sarah could see the effort Liz was putting into trying to pick up the weapon, it really did seem to be stuck. It was strange; the blade wasn't embedded in the ground or anything, and Sarah couldn't see any reason why it wouldn't be possible to pick it up.

Sarah tried to move towards Liz, but she was suddenly grabbed from behind; she attempted to elbow her assailant but missed spectacularly, stumbling backwards and losing her footing. She fell on top of the zombie, who lost her grip on Sarah. Sarah scrambled to her feet, jumping away from her attacker. She looked around frantically and counted fourteen zombies. Dónal was now trying to pick up the sword, but he, like Liz, didn't seem to be able to make it

New Girl

move in the slightest. Sarah took a deep breath and ran to his aid, picking up the sword swiftly and easily. It wasn't stuck; it just wouldn't respond to anyone but her. How come she was able to pick it up? Why did she have to be the special one? She felt a cold hand on her shoulder; spinning around, she plunged the sword into her assailant's chest, but the zombie was undeterred and kept moving forward, walking further into the blade, not seeming to care that he was being impaled as he went. The creature reached for her head with both arms; Sarah pulled the sword out of his abdomen and chopped the zombie in half, just as she had done to the other one earlier that day; the bottom half turned to bone and the top half was left on the ground, writhing and screaming. She heard Liz scream from behind her and she wished her friends could get it together. They could deal with their shock and fear later; right now, they were fighting for their lives. They needed to stay calm, to stay focused. They were both outnumbered and outclassed, and the only thing they could use to their advantage at this point was their wits. Even the seemingly-magical sword didn't seem all that useful now, although she had to admit that she felt a lot safer now that the zombie in front of her had no lower body.

"Sarah!" yelled Liz, "Help me!"

Sarah spun around just in time to see a tall, powerfully-built zombie hit Liz squarely over the head with his clenched fist; Liz slumped straight to the ground. Her eyes were closed and her body lay still; Sarah was certain that she was alive, but she certainly wasn't conscious. Dónal rushed forward and tackled the zombie in question, but the creature just struck him aside; Dónal hit the ground with a sickening thud. For a moment, Sarah feared that he, too, had been knocked unconscious, but he struggled to his feet and rushed at the zombie

New Girl

again, this time pushing the creature to the ground.

"Sarah!" he yelled. Sarah grabbed the sword and ran to Dónal's aid, and Dónal held the zombie down while she systematically chopped off its four limbs; Dónal shuddered as he watched them turn to bare bone. Sarah had only just finished chopping up the zombie when she was grabbed from behind by four hands; she spun around and jabbed at her two undead assailants, but one of them pushed her to the ground and the sword fell once again out of her grip.

It was then, while she was lying on the ground, that she saw him; the young man she had seen earlier in the school grounds. He rushed into the melée with an axe and, in one smooth blow, chopped off the heads of the two zombies who had attacked Sarah. Both bodies and heads turned to bone and fell to the ground; the creatures had been slain. Without their heads, it seemed, they could not live, or whatever it was they were doing. The distinction between dead and alive was getting blurrier and blurrier in Sarah's eyes, and she wasn't really sure she understood the nature of anything anymore.

The man helped Sarah to her feet; she began to stammer her thanks, but already he was gone, wielding his axe at another of the remaining eleven creatures, which he chopped in half but did not manage to kill.

Sarah chopped the legs off another two zombies, leaving eight whole creatures. The strange man killed another one; Sarah tried to chop off the head of yet another but she missed and only scraped its cheek. The man came to her rescue and killed the zombie. Another one grabbed him from behind, but he seemed ready for it; he elbowed it in the stomach, swung around and chopped

New Girl

off its head, littering the field with even more bones.

And then there were five against three. Five zombies against two teenagers and a strange man whose name they did not know. Liz still lay unconscious on the ground.

"She's alive," muttered Dónal to Sarah, sidling up to her, "I checked her pulse. What do we do now?"

"I don't know," snapped Sarah, "How am I supposed to know?"

Dónal didn't answer.

Darkness was rapidly falling, and Sarah began to realise that the blue glow that separated the zombies from the living was fading. Did they only glow by the light of the sun? Would anything separate them from the living once darkness fell? Would she be able to tell who was a zombie and who was not? They didn't look human, but she began to realise that the only reason for this was the blue glow; their features, their expressions, were all disarmingly akin to those of the living. Without the blue glow they would be able to blend in seamlessly.

She took a quick glance at the stranger in their midst; she estimated that he was about twenty years old. He had unkempt black hair and sallow skin, and was of slightly below average height. He didn't look as though he would be of much use in a fight, but, of course, he had already proven otherwise; Sarah would probably be dead by now had he not intervened. She wondered who he was. His accent was Irish, unlike the accent of the other strange man. Did the two men know each other? Were they working together? Had they been taking it in turns to keep tabs on her, was that why she had only seen one of them at a time?

She realised that she didn't have time to think, time to question anything. The zombies were advancing on them, and beside her Dónal was looking around with wild eyes. He was very quickly losing his nerve, and she wasn't too sure where hers was, either. Steeling herself, she lunged forward towards one of the zombies, aiming for its head, but another of them charged at her and knocked her to the ground, scratching her across the throat with a long fingernail. Sarah put her hand to her throat and took it away again; it was covered in fresh blood.

"Don't move!" called the still-unknown man as he rushed towards Sarah, easily carrying his large, threatening-looking axe in his left hand. He skilfully beheaded both the zombie who had attacked her and the one she had tried to attack, before taking off his hoodie and tying it quite tightly around Sarah's neck.

"That should stem the bleeding for the moment," he muttered, his accent betraying a Dublin upbringing, "Are you all right?"

"Yes," said Sarah weakly, getting to her feet, "Who are you?"

"Not now," he said, "We're still in danger. The ones I've killed were the weakest, these three will be a lot more difficult. I don't know if I can kill them."

"We could trap them," said Sarah.

"Where?"

"One of those crypts in the graveyard. The doors open outwards, we could try to block them with something."

"Good plan. Can your friend over there be the bait?"

New Girl

Sarah looked dubiously at Dónal.

"Yeah, but only if he doesn't know he's bait," she said, "What do we do about her?" she continued, indicating Liz, still unconscious on the ground.

"You take your red-haired friend and chase the zombies into the crypt. I'll get her to safety. Be careful, and don't do anything stupid."

Musing that trying to trick the undead was probably the very definition of stupid, Sarah ran towards Dónal as the man knelt down next to Liz.

"Trust me," Sarah said to Dónal, "Calm down, keep your cool and do exactly what I tell you to do. Otherwise we're all dead."

She hoped Dónal had some confidence in her; she knew for certain that she herself had none. She had tried her best to sound convincing, but she certainly hadn't convinced herself of anything. There was every chance this plan would fail. Still, it was the only plan they had, the only thing that stood between them and certain death. She glanced around; the zombies were coming closer and closer. She didn't have much time. It was now or never.

Chapter 11

After muttering a quick and somewhat abridged explanation of her vague plan to Dónal, Sarah charged at the zombies, turning their attention away from Liz and the still-unknown man crouched beside her. Dónal obediently followed Sarah, and the zombies leapt towards them, their faces twisted into expressions of hate mixed with glee. Sarah glanced around; Liz and the man were now nowhere to be seen. She didn't know where they had gone, but she knew that her haphazard diversion had worked. Now she just needed to take the zombies themselves out of the equation.

She started to run through the field, back in the direction of the graveyard. She leapt over a low wall, followed slightly more clumsily by Dónal, and ran with him by her side into the middle of the still-deserted graveyard, placing herself right out in the open, not caring that she trod on the resting paces of the dead; after the past two days, the dead no longer seemed so sacred. No matter how kind and scrupulous they had been in life, it seemed they were all demons when raised in this manner, and each and every corpse buried here presumably had the potential to become one of those hellish creatures. She looked to her right; the thick, stone door of the mausoleum out of which she had run was still open, swaying slightly in the wind.

"Run in there," she said to Dónal, indicating towards the crypt.

"What?" he asked incredulously, "Are you trying to kill me?"

"Just trust me," she said, "Run in there and run to the door at the opposite end. Press yourself against it but don't open it. I'll come around and get you."

"But-"

New Girl

"Just do it!" snapped Sarah as the zombies edged closer to them. Dónal ran towards the crypt after one final rueful glance at Sarah; she fervently hoped she wasn't making a terrible mistake and sending him to his death. She longed for a world where she had no huge responsibilities, for the world she had inhabited until so very recently. Two of the zombies ran after Dónal, the other, a tall and powerfully-built young man, continuing to advance on Sarah. She watched out of the corner of her eye as Dónal went into the crypt and the two zombies followed him, and she then ran after them. Just when she reached the door, she neatly side-stepped it; the zombie who was chasing her ran inside. Realising its mistake, it turned around instantly, but Sarah slammed the door shut and wedged the blade of the sword into the handle and a crevice in the side of one of the stones that made up the outer wall of the crypt; the door was now stuck. She ran around to the other end of the crypt; she could hear Dónal's cries for help from inside. She tugged on the door handle and it pulled open easily; she pulled Dónal out and slammed the door shut, trapping the three zombies inside.

"Go get something heavy," she whispered to Dónal, "Something to block the door. Quick."

She pressed her body against the door, fighting the enormous pressure coming from inside, as Dónal ran away to look for something to use. The zombies were strong. Sarah had the advantage of not being in a cramped space, but she knew the zombies would overcome her if Dónal didn't return with something usable soon. She pushed harder and harder, sweating more and more, breaking into tears of pain, the rough stone of the door cutting into her palms.

And then Dónal was there; out of the corner of her eye, she could see him

New Girl

lugging a heavy tombstone. He dragged it across the grass, finally reaching the door. Sarah stepped back, her hands still on the door, as Dónal pushed the stone in front of the door; he grabbed Sarah's arm and the two began to run.

Neither of them spoke until they were back at Drumoolly, on the road outside the farm where Liz lived. By now, night had fallen in earnest, and Sarah feared nothing more than another zombie attack. Were there more out there, or had that been it?

"Come on," said Dónal, "Liz's parents are away for the weekend, we'll go into her house. We need to do something about that cut on your neck."

Sarah's hand involuntarily went to her throat, where the man's sweater was still tied. She felt a sudden rush of nausea.

"How will we get in?" she asked.

New Girl

"I know where they keep the spare key; it's under a flowerpot."

She followed Dónal down the laneway and towards the house, the sound of her feet on the stones below louder in her ears than it should have been, becoming increasingly aware of a certain dizziness in her head. Perhaps the cut on her neck was worse than she had thought. She must be losing blood. Her head felt horribly hollow, and Dónal seemed further away than she knew him to be.

The house in front of her started to move, swaying left and right, and there appeared to be some kind of cloudy film in front of it. Black dots began to appear on the film, and then everything was gone.

Chapter 12

"Sarah. Sarah. Sarah. Sarah. Sarah. Sarah, wake up. Sarah."

She opened her eyes. Dónal's large, spotty face loomed in front of her. She appeared to be lying down on a cold, tiled floor, and the bright lights coming from the ceiling hurt her eyes.

"You're awake," said Dónal unnecessarily, "Good."

Sarah put her hand to her neck; the jumper wasn't there anymore, instead her wound was thickly bandaged.

"I don't think you're bleeding anymore," said Dónal, "at least not badly, but you lost a lot of blood on the way here."

Sitting up, Sarah saw the strange man's hoodie nearby. It was covered in congealing blood. Looking at it and knowing that the blood had come out of her made her feel sick; she looked towards Dónal instead.

"How long was I unconscious?"

"Twenty, maybe twenty-five minutes," he said, "Stay lying down. I've locked all the doors and windows and I've turned on all the lights. We should at least have a decent amount of warning if we're attacked."

"What about Liz, and that guy? Where are they?"

"Dunno. Who was he?"

"I've no idea. I was hoping you'd know."

"I'm glad he was there, anyway," said Dónal, "We'd all be dead otherwise. Look, what are we supposed to do? Should I call the guards?"

New Girl

"And what?" asked Sarah, "Tell them we're under siege from the undead? Seriously?"

"Good point."

Sarah ran her hands through her hair.

"Do you reckon Liz has her phone on her?" she asked.

"Probably," he said, "It's worth a try."

Sarah dug her own phone out of her pocket; she had five missed calls.

"Damn," she said, "My mam's been calling me. She's going to kill me."

"Not if the zombies kill you first," said Dónal helpfully. Sarah made a face at him.

"What's Liz's number?"

New Girl

Before Dónal had a chance to answer, there was a loud crash at the back door. Dónal swore.

"Too late. Can you stand?" he asked urgently, "I think we'd better go upstairs into one of the bedrooms and barricade the door."

Sarah looked up and saw large, threatening shadows looming outside the door. She stumbled to her feet; she was dizzy, but not so much that she would faint again. She had to stay conscious. She had to run, to get away. She had to stay alive.

"Come on," said Dónal, pulling her along.

"Dónal!" shrieked a voice from the dark abyss on the other side of the door. Sarah looked at Dónal.

"It's Liz," she said.

New Girl

Dónal rushed to the back door and unlocked and opened it as Sarah weakly sat back down on the floor, trying very hard not to faint again. Liz and the strange man almost fell in, and Liz slammed the door shut behind her.

"Give me the key," she said to Dónal urgently; he did so, and she frantically locked the door.

"Are they following you?" Dónal asked.

"No," said the stranger, "but there are plenty more out there. It's a bad idea to be outside right now."

"Who are you?" asked Sarah.

"I'm on your side," he said shortly, peering out the back door into the darkness.

"That's not what I asked," she said, trying not to sound as weak as she felt, "What's your name? What are you doing here?"

New Girl

"Martin, and I'm saving your life, in case you hadn't noticed. Where's your sword?"

"It's all that's keeping those creatures locked in the crypt," she said.

"Damn," said Martin, "We need to go, we need to get it back."

"Are you insane? You said we couldn't go out there!"

"This is important," said Martin, "I tried to find you earlier, to explain things to you, but you ran away. My dad said you'd be difficult to pin down for a conversation."

"Your dad?"

"Yes, my dad. The man who entrusted you with a sword forged thousands of years ago."

Suddenly, everything was falling into place. She had, however, hitherto assumed that the Australian man had only just arrived in Ireland; if he had an Irish son, he must have been here for quite some time.

"He didn't tell me it was that important," she said, sounding hurt.

"From the sound of things, you didn't let him. I'll call him now and let him know where we are, and then the two of us need to go out and get the sword."

"Me?" squeaked Sarah.

"Yes," sighed Martin, "Unfortunately, since my dad made the mistake of entrusting it to you, you're the only living being who can pick it up."

"Living being," repeated Liz, "Does that mean the zombies can pick it up?"

"Yes," said Martin, "and they're not zombies. They're the Awakened."

"The who?" asked Dónal.

New Girl

Martin sighed again, clearly growing weary of being the one with all the knowledge.

"I'll let my dad explain it when he gets here," he said, "He had to go to Wexford to investigate some possible paranormal activity, he should be back by midnight. Liz, when do your parents get back?"

"Not until Sunday," she said, "We have the house to ourselves."

"That's good," he said, "Listen, I need to phone my dad. Can I go into that room?" He pointed at a closed door, and Liz nodded.

Once he had gone, Liz turned to Sarah.

"I still haven't a clue what's going on," she said.

New Girl

"Neither do I," protested Sarah, still sitting on the floor, still seeing floating spots in front of her. Liz sat down next to her, and Dónal paced rapidly up and down, his hands trembling visibly.

"I can't believe this is happening," he said, "Zombies are real?"

Neither Liz nor Sarah said anything.

"Do you reckon they knew?" asked Liz quietly after a long silence.

"What?" asked Sarah, not quite following her train of thought.

"Theresa and Pat, before they were killed. Do you reckon they knew that the things attacking them were zombies? Or did it just happen so quickly they didn't realise?"

She buried her face in her knees and began to sob; Sarah reached out awkwardly to put a hand on her shoulder, but then thought better of it.

New Girl

She hadn't known that couple, she couldn't understand what Liz was going through, and she somehow felt at least partly responsible for the whole thing. There was nothing she could say or do that would help in the slightest; any such efforts would most likely make Liz feel worse.

"Ms Bell was there," said Dónal hollowly.

Sarah looked up.

"What?"

"The zombies we locked in the crypt; Ms Bell, the French teacher, she was one of them."

Sarah put her hand to her mouth.

"She wasn't in today," she said, "Class was cancelled." She felt sick; at the time, she had been relieved that the class was cancelled; it had never occurred to her

New Girl

that Ms Bell might be dead, or worse, undead.

There was a loud crash at the door into the adjoining room, and Martin came running into the kitchen, his eyes wild with terror.

"They're here," he yelled, "In the house, they're here. The Awakened are here."

Zombie Killers

Season 1

Sarah Reilly	Rachael Morgan	Jenny Masterson
New Girl	Changed	Body Count
First Kill	Murdered	Night Shift
Study Hall	Hated	Grave Robber
Play Dead	Loved	Mortal Enemy
True You	Risen	Small Town
No Blood	Sunken	Big Girl
Long Night	Shunned	Rotten Teeth
Young Feast	Spurned	Crushed Bones
Dark House	Taken	Empty Shell
Slow Death	Eaten	Lost Hunter

Indigo Lagoon Publications

6935513R00092

Printed in Germany
by Amazon Distributi
GmbH, Leipzig